THE INCH BOY

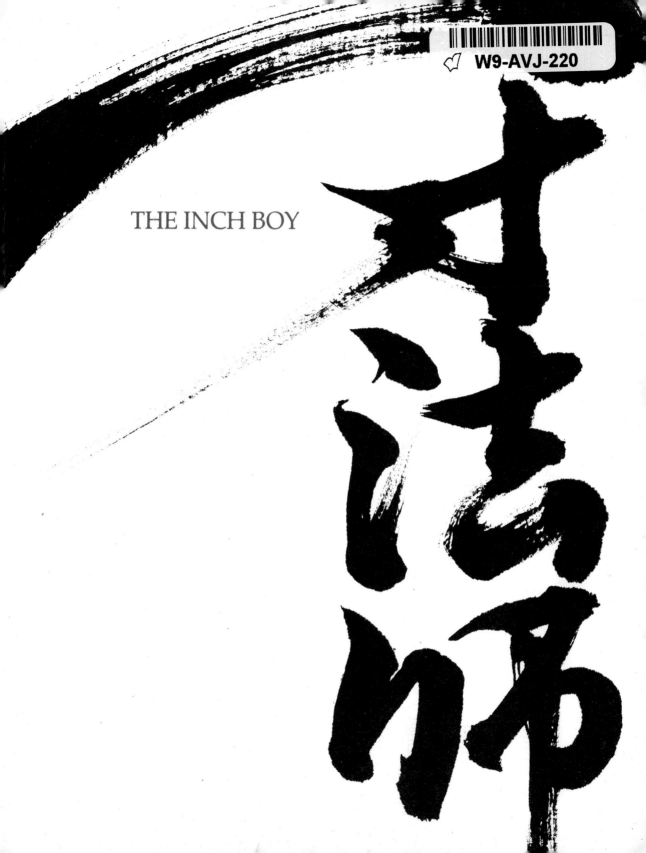

For
Bett, Eric and Peter

PUFFIN BOOKS
Viking Penguin Inc., 40 West 23rd Street, New York, New York 10010, U.S.A.
Penguin Books Ltd, 27 Wrights Lane, London W8 5TZ (Publishing & Editorial) and
Harmondsworth, Middlesex, England (Distribution & Warehouse)
Penguin Books Australia Ltd, Ringwood, Victoria, Australia
Penguin Books Canada Limited, 2801 John Street, Markham, Ontario, Canada L3R 1B4
Penguin Books (N.Z.) Ltd, 182–190 Wairau Road, Auckland 10, New Zealand

First published in Australia by William Collins Pty Ltd, 1984
First American edition published by Viking Penguin Inc., 1986
Published in Picture Puffins 1988
Illustrations copyright © Junko Morimoto, 1984
Adaptation copyright © Helen Smith, 1984
All rights reserved
Printed in Japan by Dai Nippon Printing Co., Ltd.
Set in Palatino

Library of Congress Cataloging-in-Publication Data
Smith, Helen.   The inch boy.
Adaptation of: Issun-boshi / Helen Smith.
Summary: An inch-high boy proves himself a warrior by
vanquishing the dreaded giant red demon with his cunning and bravery.
[1. Folklore—Japan] I. Morimoto, Junko, ill. II. Title.
PZ8.1.S65In 1986   398.2'1'0952 [E]   87-20967   ISBN 0-14-050677-2

The Inch Boy

illustrated by
Junko Morimoto

Puffin Books

Long ago, in Japan,
a gentle old couple
went to the temple every week.
Kneeling before
the towering Buddha,
they would ask him
to bless them with a child.

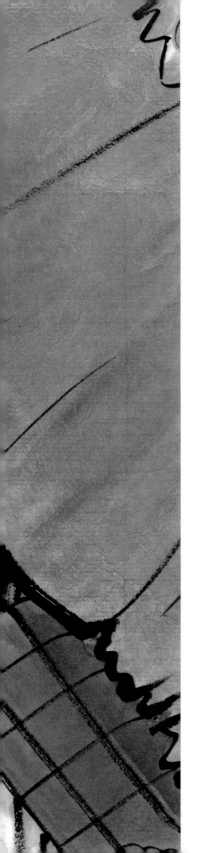

One morning they heard
a baby crying outside their home.
The old couple
glanced at each other hopefully,
"Perhaps the great Buddha
has answered our prayer
at last."
They slid open the door,
there on the step was a tiny baby.
In fact,
he was only one inch long!
With great joy the old couple
carried him into their home.
They called him Issunboshi,
little inch boy.

The years passed happily
but Issunboshi didn't grow at all.
Although he was
only one inch tall
he had the heart of a lion.
His parents' small garden
was a constant source of adventure
for Issunboshi,
but his great ambition
was to become a Samurai
and serve a noble Lord in Kyoto.

Undeterred by his size
Issunboshi was determined
to fulfil his ambition.
The quickest way to Kyoto
was by river.
Issunboshi set off
in a boat made from a rice bowl.
His paddle was one
of his mother's chopsticks.
As he set off
he looked back at his parents
on the river bank.
It was a very sad day for them
but their hearts
were full of pride
for their little Issunboshi.

Issunboshi was very excited
when the river finally
brought him to Kyoto.
"Ah! This is where I belong!"
he exclaimed.
"Here I can prove myself
to be a brave
and trusted Samurai."

Issunboshi immediately set off
for the palace
of the famous Lord Sanjo.
It took some time
before he managed to attract
the attention of the guard
at the huge wooden gates.
"I am Issunboshi,"
he announced.
"I have heard many tales
of the great Lord Sanjo
and it is my wish to serve
such an honourable man.
Please sir,
announce my arrival."

The guard was so surprised
that he called
Lord Sanjo's attendants
to inspect Issunboshi.
Issunboshi looked very commanding
as he stood before them.
In his hand
he clasped the sewing needle
that his mother had given him
for a sword.
Feeling they had no alternative
but to obey,
the attendants presented Issunboshi
to Lord Sanjo.

Issunboshi was appointed
special bodyguard
to Princess Makiko,
Lord Sanjo's daughter.
It was a beautiful spring day.
Cherry blossoms
framed the ancient city.
Princess Makiko and her entourage
were returning from an outing
to the famous Kiyomizu temple.
Suddenly the sky darkened . . .

. . . and out of a terrifying wind
stepped a giant Red Demon.
He had come
to capture the Princess.
Swish . . . swish . . .
went the Samurais' swords,
but the giant Red Demon
was too strong.
Helpless and disarmed,
they all fled in terror.
Only Issunboshi stood his ground.
"I am Issunboshi,"
he shouted up to the giant.
"I will destroy you!
Prepare yourself Red Demon!"

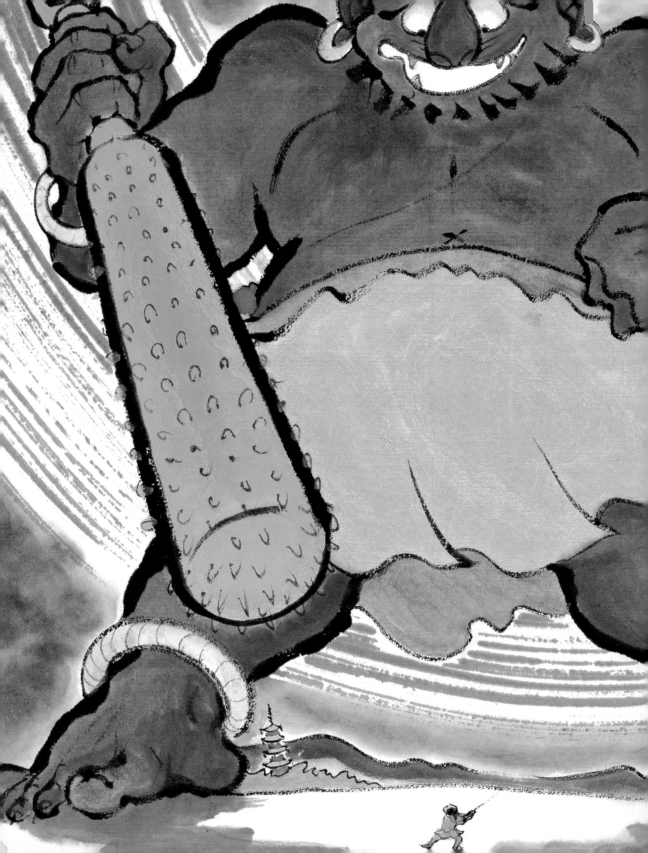

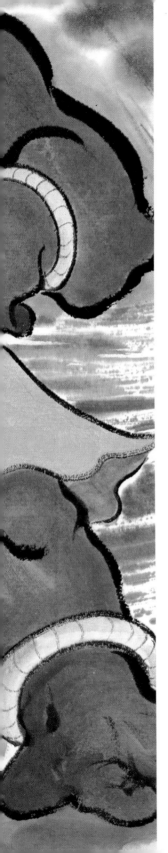

When the giant Red Demon
saw who was speaking,
he scooped Issunboshi up
and roared with laughter.
"You!" he bellowed.
"You are no bigger than a mouse
— and a small one at that!"

However,
Issunboshi was too quick
for the Demon.
He plunged into his mouth
and without hesitating,
ran down
into the giant's stomach.

JAB! JAB! JAB! JAB!
Here, there, everywhere,
Issunboshi thrust
his little sword.
"Ooh! Aah! Ouch!
Help, help!"
the Demon howled.
"Surrender!"
demanded the little Samurai.
"Promise that you
will never be evil again."
"Yes! Yes!
I promise, I promise,"
groaned the Red Demon.
"Please, please just come out."

With that,
Issunboshi leapt out.
The Red Demon,
clutching his aching stomach,
ran away.
In his rush to escape
from Issunboshi's tiny sword,
he dropped his magic hammer.
As Issunboshi reached out
to touch the magic hammer,
a miracle happened . . .

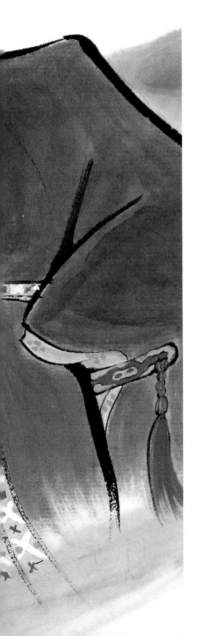

Issunboshi began to grow
. . . and grow
. . . and grow.
There he stood,
not an Issunboshi any more
but General Horikawa,
a handsome and gallant Samurai.
It wasn't long
before the news
of General Horikawa's courage
had spread throughout Japan.
Issunboshi's great ambition
was realised.
General Horikawa
and Princess Makiko were married.
Not forgetting
his loving parents,
Issunboshi invited them
to share his home
and newfound happiness in Kyoto.